# THREE STO...

## You Can Read to Your
# TEDDY BEAR

**Sara Swan Miller**   *ILLUSTRATED BY* **True Kelley**

*sandpiper*

HOUGHTON MIFFLIN HARCOURT
Boston  New York

**For Larry Kasper—
Thanks for the
inspirational teddy bear!
—S.S.M.**

**For Charlotte and
Eloise Lindblom
—T.K.**

Text copyright © 2003 by Sara Swan Miller
Illustrations copyright © 2003 by True Kelley

All rights reserved. Published in the United States by Sandpiper, an imprint of
Houghton Mifflin Harcourt Publishing Company. Originally published in hardcover in
the United States by Houghton Mifflin Books for Children, an imprint of Houghton Mifflin Harcourt
Publishing Company, 2003.

SANDPIPER and the SANDPIPER logo are trademarks of Houghton Mifflin Harcourt Publishing
Company.

For information about permission to reproduce selections from this book,
write to Permissions, Houghton Mifflin Harcourt Publishing Company,
215 Park Avenue South, New York, New York 10003.

www.hmhbooks.com

The text of this book is set in 16-point Baskerville Book.
The illustrations are ink and watercolor.

The Library of Congress has cataloged the hardcover edition as follows:
Miller, Sara Swan.
Three stories you can read to your teddy bear/by Sara Swan Miller;
illustrated by True Kelley.
p. cm.
Summary: Bored with sitting on a shelf day after day, a teddy bear sets out on
three adventures and inadvertently gets the family dog and cat in trouble.
[1. Teddy bears—Fiction 2. Adventures and adventurers—Fiction.
3. Dogs—Fiction 4. Cats—Fiction.] I. Kelley, True, ill. II Title.
PZ7.M63344Tl 2004
[Fic]—dc22
2003012428

ISBN: 978-0-618-30397-7 hardcover
ISBN: 978-0-547-74450-6 paperback

Manufactured in China
LEO 10 9 8 7 6 5 4 3 2 1
4500340731

# CONTENTS

# Introduction

Do you have a teddy bear? Most people do. You must love your teddy. But don't you think Teddy gets bored sometimes? Teddies can't walk. Teddies can't eat. Teddies can't talk. All a teddy bear can do is sit there. Poor Teddy!

What can you do to cheer up your teddy bear? You can tickle Teddy. You can invite Teddy to a tea party. You can take Teddy for a ride on your bike.

What else can you do? Here's a good idea. You can read these stories out loud. Teddy will like them a lot. Teddies like to hear about their adventures. And you may learn things you never knew about your teddy. Even a teddy bear has secrets!

Up you go, Teddy! Come sit on my lap.
Here is a story just for you.

# 1

## A GOOD
## IDEA

One morning you were sitting on the bed. You
sat on the bed every morning. What else was there
to do? Every morning your friend left you there.

Morning after morning it was the same.

"I am so tired of sitting on this bed," you said
to yourself. "Same old bed. Same old dresser.
Same old pictures on the wall. What a bore!"

You sat there feeling sorry for yourself. Then
you had an idea.

"I know," you said to yourself. "I will take a walk!"

A walk would be fun!

"But wait a minute," you said to yourself. "Everyone knows that teddies can't walk. Teddies can't even move!"

That *was* a problem. Now you felt even sorrier for yourself. You sat and sat.

Then you had another idea.

"Maybe people don't know everything about teddies," you said to yourself. "Maybe teddies *can* walk! At least I can try."

You closed your eyes and thought very hard. Then, very slowly, you raised one arm. Wow! It worked! Then you raised your other arm. That worked, too! You wiggled your right leg. You wiggled your left leg.

"Here I go," you said to yourself.
You pushed hard with your right leg.

Slowly, slowly, you rolled over, and THUD!

You landed on the floor. "Ouch!" you said.

You lay there with your nose on the hard floor.

"Well," you said at last. "I can't lie here all day. This is almost as boring as sitting on the bed."

Slowly, slowly, you rolled over. Slowly, slowly, you sat up. Slowly, slowly, you pushed yourself onto your feet.

You took a step. Then another.
"I'm walking!" you said.

Thud! Oops! You fell on your nose again.

You took a little rest there on the floor. Then you rolled over again. You sat up. You pushed yourself to your feet. You took a step, then another. You took three, four, five steps! You were really on your way now! You watched your feet walking along.

"Go, feet!" you said.

Clunk! OUCH!

What is that wall doing in the way?" you asked yourself.

Maybe it was better to let your feet do the job on their own. You held your head high and started off again. You walked down the hall. You walked very, very carefully. You didn't look at your feet even once. You looked at the ceiling instead.

"People are wrong," you said to yourself. "Teddies *can* walk!"

You took some more steps.

"But I will never tell my friend," you said. "This will be my teddy bear secret."

What? Where did the floor go? CLUMPITY, CLUMPITY, CLUMPITY, THUMPITY,

THUMP!

You fell all the way down the stairs and landed
on your nose again. You lay there for a long time.
Who knew walking would be so hard on your
nose?

"Help!" you said in a squeaky voice. "Help
and double help!"

WHUFF WHUFF WHUFF WHUFF! Here
came the dog! Maybe the dog would help. The
dog shoved at you with its big, wet nose. But it
didn't help one bit.

"I need to get upstairs,"
you said to the dog.
"What if our friend comes
home and finds me here?
What if our friend finds out
my secret?"

Uh-oh! Your friend came in the door. Your
friend had caught you!

"Bad dog!" said your friend. "Look what you did to Teddy! Go lie down, bad dog!"

Your friend picked you up and gave you a hug.

"Poor Teddy," said your friend.

Poor dog, you thought. You gave the dog a little wink.

You got a nice cuddle. Then your friend took you upstairs and put you back on the bed.

You sat there and looked at the boring dresser and the boring pictures on the wall.

"Well," you said to yourself, "it may be boring here, but at least my nose will get a rest."

You snuggled into the pillow and took a nice long rest yourself.

Why are you looking at me like that, Teddy?
Do you want to hear another story? Okay, here is
another one that you will like.

# 2

## WHAT'S FOR BREAKFAST?

The next morning your friend went away again. There you sat on the boring bed. At least your nose felt better.

"I think I will have another adventure," you said to yourself. "But this time I will be very, very careful, nose."

Very, very carefully, you slid off the bed.

Very, very carefully, you stood on your feet. Very, very carefully, you walked down the hall. You didn't look at your feet. You didn't look at the ceiling. You looked straight ahead.

You found a bedroom and another bedroom.
They were much more interesting than *your* old
bedroom. Then you found a bathroom.

"This looks like fun!" you said to yourself.

You stepped inside. Oops! Who knew the floor
was so slippery? The bathroom wasn't much fun
after all.

"Sorry, nose," you said.

Slowly, slowly, you picked yourself up. Very, very carefully, you crawled out the door. Very, very carefully, you got to your feet. There were those stairs again!

"I wonder what's down there?" you asked to yourself.

But how could you get down the stairs? There must be a better way than falling down thumpity, thumpity, CLUNK. You thought for a long time.

Then you sat down on the top
step, and bump, bump,
bump, bump, you
bumped down nicely
on your bottom.

"I'm getting to be such a smart bear," you said
to yourself.

You walked around the living room. You walked around the dining room. Then you walked all the way into the kitchen.

"What is that smell?" you asked yourself. "It's a good smell. It's a tasty smell. It's a smell that says I'M HUNGRY!"

You followed your nose. You followed it all the way to a big door.

The smell was inside!
You put your nose in the
crack and—oh, boy!
The door opened!

"Thank you, nose," you said.

Just then you heard tip, tip, tip, tip, tip. Here came the cat.

"Bad bear!" said the cat. "No bears allowed in the food closet!"

"Why not?" you said. "Here *it* is. And here *I* am. And I want breakfast!"

You reached inside and pulled out a box. It
spilled all over the floor. Was this your breakfast?
No, it was just hard little bits of white stuff.

"Stop, Teddy!" said the cat. "You are going to
get into big trouble."

You reached inside and pulled out a can. It
spilled all over the floor, too. Was this your breakfast? No, it was just some boring brown powder.

"Bad Teddy!" said the cat. "Now you are in
bigger trouble."

You reached inside the closet again. You felt all around. You felt a sticky jar and gave it a sniff. This was it!

You knocked the jar on the floor. Yummy, gooey, warm, sweet stuff spilled out. You set right to work. You licked and licked and slurped and slurped. It was a great breakfast! You licked until the jar was empty. Then you set to work licking the sticky stuff out of your fur.

"Watch out!" said the cat. "Here comes my friend. Now you are in big, BIG trouble!"

Uh-oh! This time your friend would find out your secret! You plopped down on the floor and sat very, very still.

"You bad kitty, you!" said your friend. "What have you done? Scat, cat!"

Poor cat, you thought.

Your friend picked you up. But you didn't get a cuddle this time.

"That bad cat got you all sticky," said your friend. "You need a wash."

Your friend put you in the sink. Scrub, scrub, scrub. It was nasty! But you sat very still. You didn't want your friend to know your secret. Finally, your friend was done.

"You sit here on the windowsill to dry," said your friend. "Sorry I can't put you on the bed."

"Why is my friend sorry?" you asked yourself.
"It's much nicer here!"

You sat on the sill and looked out the window.
You watched the birds swooping. You watched the
squirrels leaping in the trees.

"I wonder what else is out there," you said to
yourself. "Maybe tomorrow I will find out!"

Tomorrow would be another fun day! But now
you were very tired. You leaned back and took a
nice nap on the sunny sill.

Did you like that story, Teddy? Would you like one more? Okay, here is the very last one.

# 3

---

# THE GREAT OUTDOORS

The next morning your friend went away again. There you sat on the kitchen windowsill. The window was open. The air smelled great.

"I'm off into the great outdoors!" you said to yourself.

Very, very carefully, you climbed out the window. You held onto the sill with your paws. Then you let go.

"Oof!" you said. "The ground is hard! Sorry, nose."

But your nose didn't mind. It was too busy sniffing the air.

What was out there? You stood up and began
to walk. You walked around a bush. You walked
all around a tree. You took a nice walk through the
flower bed. Then you stopped for a while to nibble
on the flowers. Yum! You nibbled them all up.
Then off you went again.

You fell down only once! Well, twice. Okay, three times. But that's very good for a teddy bear.

"This is fun!" you said.

You walked some more.

"But I wish I had someone to play with," you said to yourself.

A bird was hopping on the lawn.

"Do you want to play with me?" you asked.
"Eek!" said the bird. "A big, bad bear!"
The bird flew away.

A squirrel was nibbling on a nut.

"Do you want to play with me?" you asked.

"Aaag!" yelled the squirrel. "A bear! A scary bear!"

"Wow!" you said to yourself. "Everyone is scared of big, scary ME!"

You stood still and felt very proud. And very big.

"But I still don't have anyone to play with," you said.

Then WHUFF WHUFF WHUFF WHUFF!
Here came the dog.

"Do you want to play with me?" you asked.

"Yes!" said the dog. "Oh yes, oh yes, oh yes!"

You played Dig Holes in the Lawn.
You played Bury Teddy
in the Flower Bed.

You played
Toss Teddy in the Air.
What fun!

"I know," you said. "You could take me for a doggy-back ride!"

You climbed on top, and away you went!

"Whee!" you said. "Faster! Faster!"

You were going like the wind.

"I am a great doggy-back rider!" you said.

Suddenly the dog stopped short. You fell headfirst on the ground. Poor nose!

Uh-oh. Here came your friend. You were in
big, big trouble now! Now your friend would
guess your secret for sure.

"You bad, bad dog, you!" said your friend.
"Look what you did to poor teddy. He is all dirty.
And you, cat! Look what you did to the flower
bed! Bad, bad dog!
Bad, bad cat!"

Your friend picked you up and took you back inside. You got another awful wash. Then your friend put you back on the windowsill to dry. You sat very still, the way a teddy bear is supposed to.

"What a great day I had," you said to yourself. "Tomorrow I will have even more fun. And my friend will NEVER guess my secret!"

You snuggled down and took a long, long nap in the warm sunshine.